For Adam, who will forever be the boy
K.W.

For my family
V.I.D.

First published in 2018 by Ditton Publishing

10864213579

Text © 2018 Karen Walker
Illustrations © 2018 Virginie Degorgue

Karen Walker and Virginie Degorgue have asserted their right
to be identified as the author and illustrator of this work under
the Copyright, Designs and Patents Act, 1988.

This book has been typeset in Palatino Linotype

Printed in Great Britain by Biddles Books Ltd.

A catalogue record for this book is available from the British Library.

ISBN 978-1-9999954-0-9

www.thesmoth.com

THE Smoth

by Karen Walker

illustrated by
Virginie Degorgue

To Scott and Charlotte
love from
William and Sarah
X X

Karen Walker   Virginie Degorgue

Ditton
PUBLISHING

A boy and his mum ride a
bike through the park.
They're trying to get home
'cause he's scared of the dark.

"No need to be scared",
said the mother to he,
"You'll always be safe
when you're riding with me".

. . . But then up from a swamp
rose the strangest of things,
with giant balloons
and the smallest of wings.

The mother she screamed
and was scared for them both,
but her son said, "Don't worry,
it's only a smoth".

. . .But oh such a creature
they never had seen,
he stood six feet tall
with a body that seemed

to be shaking all over
and covered in goo,
with a tail long and curly
and fur midnight blue.

The goo was bright green
and it fell in great globs

onto big purple feet,
as he let out great sobs.

He was out of this world,
only meant to be seen,
in a book . . .

or maybe a dream.

He had turquoise eyes
and a face that was yellow.

He climbed from the swamp
then he let out a bellow.

Orange tears oozed
and fell from his eyes
more and more,

they dropped
to the ground
and he let out a ROAR!

The mother was fearful
and said to her son,
"It's time to go home now,
but best we don't run".

"Go home", said the boy,
"but mother", said he,
"I want to know more and
I don't want to flee".

He went to the smoth
and he asked him his name.
The smoth stopped his howling
and said it was Shane.

"But why are you here
with balloons in a bog"?
"I was learning to fly
and I fell off this log".

"Fell off this log", said the boy, "is that all"?

"And . . . my body's too big

and . . . my wings are too small.

And the other smoths laugh and I'm not very brave
and I hate to be teased so I live in a cave.

All alone with no friends
and I'm really quite sad
and they all think I'm strange
when I sometimes get mad.

So I'm learning to fly,
when there's no one around,

but my wings are too small
and I fall to the ground.

Then I found these balloons,
'hoped they'd help me to fly,
but they didn't help much,
'cause I need to be high".

"I know just the thing", said the boy, "come with me,

to the edge of the swamp",
where he found Shane a tree.

Shane left from the tree
and he drifted away,
and from far in the distance
they just heard him say,

"It was lovely to meet you,
'hope to see you again,
it is so nice to know
that I've found me a friend".

So they watched while Shane
floated away in the breeze,
above all the hilltops
and over the trees.

As the sun slowly faded
and sank far away,
it was time now to leave,
everything was okay.

A boy and his mum ride
a bike through the park.
They're trying to get home
'cause she's scared of the dark.